Hi! I'm Darcy J. Doyle, Daring Detective,

but you can call me D.J. The only thing I like better than reading a good mystery is solving one. When someone sabotaged our tent on our campout, I had to do something about it. Let me tell you about The Case of the Creepy Campout.

Books in the Darcy J. Doyle,

Daring Detective series:

Darcy J. Doyle
Daring Detective

The Case of the
Creepy Campout

Linda Lee Maifair

ZondervanPublishingHouse
Grand Rapids, Michigan

A Division of HarperCollinsPublishers

The Case of the Creepy Campout
Copyright © 1994 by Linda Lee Maifair

Request for information should be addressed to:
Zondervan Publishing House
Grand Rapids, Michigan 49530

Library of Congress Cataloging-in-Publication Data

Maifair, Linda Lee.
    The case of the creepy campout / by Linda Lee Maifair.
      p cm. — (Darcy J. Doyle, daring detective : #5
    Summary: When Darcy Doyle goes camping with her
church youth group, she is hired to investigate the mysterious
noises which disturb them.
    ISBN 0-310-43271-5 (paper)
    [1. Camping—Fiction. 2. Christian life—3. Mystery and
detective stories.] I. Title. II. Series: Maifair, Linda Lee.
Darcy J. Doyle, daring detective : #5
PZ7.M2776Case 1994
[Fic]—dc20   94-4577
                                                      CIP
                                                      AC

Edited by Dave Lambert
Interior design by Rachel Hostetter
Illustrations by Tim Davis
Cover design by Anne Huizenga

Printed in the United States of America

94 95 96 97 98 99 / ❖ OP /10 9 8 7 6 5 4 3 2 1

*With special thanks to those
who have made the Darcy series a reality:*

*To Dave Lambert
for seeing the possibilities.*

*To Lori Walburg
for editing with such gentle care.*

*To Tim Davis
for bringing the stories and characters
to life with his illustrations.*

*And with gratitude to God,
for giving me the opportunity to touch the lives
of so many children.*

CHAPTER 1

I'm Darcy J. Doyle. Some of my friends call me Darcy. Some just call me D.J. If I keep on solving important cases, pretty soon everyone will be calling me Darcy J. Doyle, Daring Detective. It's only a matter of time.

My last big case started when Greg Sulinski asked Mr. Henderson if the boys in our church youth group could go camping at Pine Valley State Park.

"They've got hiking trails," Greg said, "and bike rentals, and rowboats for the lake, and big campsites where we could pitch our tents and have a campfire."

He made it sound like so much fun, the girls decided they wanted to go too. "It would make a *great* retreat," my best friend Mandy Thompson told Mrs. Henderson. The Hendersons and my parents were co-leaders of the upper-elementary youth group.

"*Girls*? Camping?" Nick Rinaldi said. He laughed, and all the boys in the group laughed with him.

"Why not?" I said. "Girls can camp just as well as boys."

"You'd be scared stiff," Greg said.

"Of what?" I asked.

"Bears," Nick said. "And snakes."

"And sleeping in the woods," Greg added. "And — "

I was sorry I'd asked. "*Ha!*" I interrupted, hoping I sounded more convincing than I felt.

"Boys and girls!" my mother said. She was looking right at me. "We're here for fellowship, not fighting."

I thought for sure that was the end of the camping idea. But my father surprised me. "You know," he said, "maybe a camping retreat would be a good idea. In camp, everybody would have to pitch in and help out just to get meals ready and keep the fire going. Maybe it would teach us to pull together instead of pulling apart."

Pitching in, helping out, pulling together, learning lessons — that didn't sound like nearly as much fun as hiking, biking, boating, and building campfires. But the kids all voted to go to Pine Valley anyway.

All except Tricia Norton, that is. Tricia had one objection after another.

"It'll be *cold* out there this time of year.

"It's a *two-hour* drive to Pine Valley. I get car-sick.

"I don't *like* campfire food.

"The ground is too *hard*. I'll never be able to sleep!

"My mother won't let me go."

By that time, I was praying that she was right — that her mother *wouldn't* let her go.

At our next meeting, we made plans for the campout. Dad said he'd ask the local Boy Scout troop if we could borrow a few of their tents for the weekend. We planned our menus. We figured out how much everyone would need to pitch in for the food. We talked about what we should wear and what we should bring along.

Thinking about the dark woods, the bears, and the snakes, I said, "I think we should bring my faithful bloodhound, Max."

"Max?" everybody said at the same time.

I nodded. "For protection." I ignored the laughter. "Max is a fierce and fearless watchdog," I said.

"Yeah," Nick said. "He'd watch a crook take everything."

"And he'd watch from behind a tree," Greg added.

Before I could give them one of my looks, Dad surprised me again. "Actually," he said, "taking Max might not be such a bad idea. He's got a bark that would scare away anybody who didn't know him. And he'd bark at anybody he didn't know."

Tricia Norton, whose mother had told her she could go after all, complained again. "I don't *like* dogs," she said. "They make me itch."

Everyone but Tricia voted to take Max along.

Two weeks later, four adult leaders, fourteen excited kids, one itchy complainer, and one very big dog gathered in the church parking lot to load up and head out. Nick Rinaldi introduced Mandy and me to his brother, who had given him a ride to the church.

"This is my brother, Barry," Nick said. "And his friend Joel." He nodded at the scrawny black kitten Barry was holding. "And that's Poe, our new cat."

"Neat name," I said. "Like Edgar Allan Poe?"

Barry shrugged. "My father named him."

I tried to make conversation. "Nick says you guys go camping a lot," I said.

"Yeah," Barry said. "Nothing like it. Hiking in the hills. Cooking steaks over an open fire. Sleeping under the stars." He gave me a funny smile. "You sure you girls won't be afraid —

12

out there in the woods with all those creepy-crawlies?"

Hmmmm. So Nick had told him about our argument. That bugged me. And it bugged me even more that Barry was teasing us about it. I was sorry I'd tried making conversation after all. "Sure I'm sure!" I told him.

He was still smiling his funny smile when the bus pulled out of the parking lot. "He's as bad as Nick," Mandy whispered. I nodded.

On the way to Pine Valley State Park, we had to pull over four times to let Tricia Norton throw up in the bushes beside the road.

Of course Greg and Nick thought it was hilarious. "That's what happens when you take *girls* camping!" Nick laughed.

CHAPTER 2

All the campsites had names from books. Ours was called Sleepy Hollow.

"*You* know," I told Mandy, "like in that story we read in school? About Ichabod Crane and the Headless Horseman?"

"Ooooh!" Tricia Norton squealed, loudly. "That story was *creepy*." She looked over her shoulder, first in one direction, then the other. "This place is creepy too. Do you think it's *safe* here?"

"Oh, *please!*" Carol Wilson threw her backpack on the ground next to the pile of tent stakes Dad had given us.

"Humpf!" Mandy muttered. She gave the pile of canvas in front of her — our tent — a good hard kick.

There was a reason Mandy and Carol were in a bad mood. We'd been divided into groups of four. Carol, Mandy, and I ended up with Tricia Norton.

"Nobody else wants her," my mother had told Mandy and Carol and me. "It'll be an act of Christian charity."

"It'll be a pain," Carol had whispered. Mandy and I had agreed.

I looked across the clearing to where Greg, Nick, Jon, and Tony were unfolding their own tent. "Come on," I told Mandy and Carol. I started laying out the canvas on the ground. "I don't want us to be the last ones done."

16

When my dad was a kid, he was a Boy Scout and went camping all the time. So he had shown us all how to pitch the tents — how to lay out the canvas, where to put the stakes, how to prop it up and tie it down. "Nothing to it," he had said. He'd made it look easy.

Greg and Nick, who did a lot of camping with their brothers, had their tent up in no time. But even with Max's help, ours didn't go up quite as well.

Mandy, Carol, and I heaved and tugged at the canvas. "Get off of it, Max! Let go of it!"

We hammered at the stakes. "Bring that back, Max! We're not here to play fetch!"

We got tangled up in the lines. "Max! Stop! Your tail is tied to the tent post!"

Finally, our arms aching from pulling and our palms burning from the ropes, we stood back to examine our work.

Our tent leaned to the left and sagged in the middle. I leaned to my left and cocked my head sideways. "Looks good to me," I said.

"Not bad," Carol agreed.

"I knew we could do it," Mandy said.

"Woof! Woof!" Max said proudly.

Tricia Norton got up off the bedroll she'd been sitting on the whole time. "One little puff of wind and it's going to blow away," she said, shaking her head. "It's going to come crashing down on our heads in the middle of the night." She waved a hand at the other tents around the clearing. "It doesn't look anything like those," she said. And on and on she went, complaining.

Mandy, Carol, and I picked up our backpacks and sleeping bags and crawled into the tent. Max went with us.

"What a pain," Carol said again.

18

"Why didn't she just stay home?" Mandy grumbled.

"I don't want that dog in my tent!" Tricia whined, sticking her head inside the tent flap just as I pulled a bag of chocolate-chip cookies out of my backpack. "And you shouldn't eat in here," she nagged. "All sorts of creepy-crawly creatures will be after the crumbs. They'll carry us off in the middle of the night."

The thought of Tricia being carried off by creepy-crawly creatures made me grin. I pulled out a cookie and offered it to Max.

He was happy to get it. A little *too* happy. He wagged his tail left and right. Hard. It thumped against one of the tent poles. Swat. Swat. *Swat! Crash!*

Three girls and a very large dog thrashed around under the canvas, trying to find the tent flap in the dark.

"Crawl over this way. Ouch! Watch your elbows!"

"No, it's over here! Max, get your tail out of my face!"

"Wait! Don't anybody move! I think I lost a contact lens!"

From outside the tent came a nagging voice: "I *told* you that dog shouldn't be in the tent! I *told* you it was going to fall down. I *knew* this campout was a bad idea!"

"Woof! Woof!"

Rip.

Growl.

"*Helllllp!*"

Help came quickly. Most of it was laughing. Some of it was even taking pictures.

CHAPTER 3

The noises started about midnight. Soft and low and creepy, right behind our tent.

Ooooooooo! Screeeeech! Scraaatch!

"D.J.?" Mandy whispered. "Are you awake?"

I was. And it wasn't the spooky stories the boys had told around the campfire that had been keeping me awake. I'd been lying there eating chocolate-chip cookies, thinking about how Dad had helped us out of our tent when it had fallen down. And how Greg had stood there laughing. And how Nick had taken pictures of the whole thing! It was humiliating.

Skitter. Hiss! Yoowwll!

Mandy sat up on one side of me. Carol sat up on the other. I stayed scrunched down in my sleeping bag in between. "What *is* that?" Carol asked.

I had no idea. But it had sounded close.

Howwwlll! Ruff! Ruff! Howwll!

That sound I knew. It was our fierce and fearless watchdog, Max. We'd left him tied to a tent stake in the middle of the campsite. As far as I was concerned, Max should have been inside the tent and somebody *else* should have been outside.

I could hear Carol feeling around her in the dark. "Where's Tricia?" she whispered, as if she'd been reading my mind.

"Who cares," Mandy said.

I smiled. "Maybe a bunch of creepy-crawly creatures carried her — " I didn't get to finish.

23

"Auuggh!" Carol screamed. She struggled to stand up in her sleeping bag.

Something padded across my legs and headed for Mandy. "Auuggh!" I echoed Carol. I tried to unzip my sleeping bag and stand up beside her.

"Auuggh!" Mandy joined the chorus of yelps and squeals.

I couldn't get my sleeping bag undone. Neither could the others. We hopped toward the tent flap like three kids in a sack race. Mandy first. Then me. Then Carol.

Something made angry little hissing noises and tried to climb up my sleeping bag. "Auuggh!" I pushed Mandy toward the flap.

Mandy fell to her knees, unzipped the tent flap, and crawled out, still in her sleeping bag. Like a caterpillar in a cocoon, I wriggled out behind her with Carol close at my heels, and then I tried to stand up. "Auuggh!"

Something large and furry thumped against my chest, knocking me to the ground. Something big and heavy stood over me, pinning my shoulders down. Something warm and wet slurped across my face. "Woof! Woof!" Something big bounded off toward the tent.

"No, Max!" I yelled. It was too late.

Yowlll! Ruff! Hiss! Screech! Growl! Crash!

Flashlight beams and running footsteps approached from all directions. A camera flash went off in my face. Boys' laughter rang in my ears.

"There was something in our tent!" I told my mother.

"Something *big*!" Mandy said. She held her hands about three feet off the ground and three feet apart.

Carol nodded. "Something *furry*!" she added.

"I *told* them not to eat in the tent, Mrs. Doyle! I told them, but they wouldn't listen!"

I wasn't all that relieved to find out that the creepy-crawly creatures hadn't taken Tricia Norton after all. I was sorely tempted to tell her so.

"It attacked us!" I told my mother. I pointed to the wriggling, growling, hissing heap of canvas a few feet away. "Our fierce and fearless watchdog came to rescue us. Max went right into the tent after it!" I turned to my father. "You've got to save him, Dad!"

Dad and Mr. Henderson got a couple of big sticks and slowly approached the tent. It took them a while to find the opening and let Max out. He came out with his tail between his legs and the chocolate-chip cookie bag in his mouth.

"Some fierce and fearless watchdog!" Greg said.

"At least he rescued the cookies," Nick joined in.

Dad and Mr. Henderson searched the remains of the tent. There was no sign of the huge, furry creature that had attacked us. "It was probably just a raccoon or a squirrel — after the cookies," Mr. Henderson suggested.

Dad was sitting back on his heels, staring at the tent he was pitching for us for the second time. "This doesn't look like a raccoon or squirrel to me, Tom," he told Mr. Henderson.

Mr. Henderson, Mrs. Henderson, Mom, and all us kids peered down to where Dad's flashlight beam shone on the side of the tent. One of the seams was coming apart. "No animal did this," Dad said. "This has been cut on purpose."

Mrs. Henderson shook her head. "But why would somebody cut open their tent?" she said.

It didn't take long for my daring detective mind to figure it out. "So that somebody could put that — that *creature* — in our tent and scare us half to death!"

"Who would want to do something like that?" Mrs. Henderson said.

"I want to go home! I want to go home right now!" Tricia Norton wailed.

It took Mrs. Henderson an hour to get her quiet.

The next morning, between prayers and pancakes, my mother handed me two dollars.

"What's this for?" I asked.

"It's your fee," Mom said. "I want to know who's responsible for what happened last night." She gave me a hug. "So I'm hiring the best detective I know."

CHAPTER 4

It was my dad's idea to pair us off, boy-girl, boy-girl, for the morning hike. And I knew he put me with Nick Rinaldi on purpose. He wanted us to learn to "pull together."

Throughout the hike, partners were supposed to walk together and eat together. It was okay with me. After all, now I was on a case. Having Nick as a partner would give me a chance to start my investigation.

When we stopped for a fruit-and-rest break, I sat down on a rock and emptied my fanny pack. Nick sat down on a log a couple of feet away. Mandy and her hike partner, Greg Sulinski, came over and sat by us — Mandy next to me and Greg next to Nick.

Nick unzipped the jacket he was wearing. "Wish I'd remembered to bring a sweatshirt," he told Greg. "This jacket's too warm, and it's too cold to go without it."

He glanced over at me and saw my notebook and pencil. "What's that for?" he asked.

"Where were you last night — " I started to ask him.

Mandy interrupted me with a big smile. "You're on a *case*, aren't you, Darcy! You're going to find out who caused all that trouble last night, aren't you?" She turned to Nick and Greg. "D.J.'s a great detective, you know."

Nick laughed. "Yeah, we know. She tells us all the time."

I gave him one of my looks and tried to repeat my question. "Where were you last night — "

"With everybody else," he interrupted. "Watching that dog of yours rescue your cookie bag!" He and Greg broke up laughing.

Ordinarily, I might have bopped them, but daring detectives can't go around bopping suspects no matter how annoying they were. "Where were you *before* that?" I asked. "When those creepy noises started and that — that *thing* came into our tent?"

Nick looked at Greg. "We were in our tent. Sleeping. Weren't we."

Greg nodded. "Yeah," he said. He was looking at Nick, not at me. "Sleeping."

Neither one sounded all that convincing. I scribbled in my notebook:

Suspects: Nick and Greg.

Motive: To scare us.

Alibi: Sleeping.

Clues:

Hmmm. I had no clues. "What woke you up?" I asked Greg.

He smiled. "All that screeching you girls were doing." He demonstrated. "Auugggh!"

"And that dog, barking and howling," Nick added. He barked and howled.

I stared at my notebook. "Hmmmm," I said. Daring detectives always say "hmmmm" when they're thinking. It also comes in handy when you're trying not to bop somebody and you don't have anything better to say.

It made Nick curious. He came over to look at my notes. "What did you write about us?" He reached for the notebook. I yanked it away and tried to stuff it into my fanny pack, but Nick grabbed my wrist. "Let me see what you're writing about me, Darcy Doyle!"

I tried to pull away from him. "Leave me alone, Nick Rinaldi!"

"Ahem!" The sound of a throat clearing impatiently behind us made both of us jump.

"Uh, Dad!" I gave him what I hoped was an innocent smile. "We were just . . ."

Dad smiled too, but it wasn't the sort of smile that made you feel very confident. "Nick and Darcy!" he said. "How nice of the two of you to volunteer to give the message before prayers tonight."

"But, Mr. Doyle, we didn't — " Nick protested.

"I think something on cooperation would be appropriate," Dad said.

"But, Dad — "

"Don't worry." Dad grinned. "I'm sure you'll do a great job if you work together."

CHAPTER 5

"I think you're on the wrong track," Mandy told me at lunch.

Carol Wilson agreed. "We think it was Tricia."

Tricia? I tried to imagine Tricia Norton crawling around in the dark, making noises and stuffing some wild creature into our tent. "You've got to be kidding!"

Carol shook her head. "She wasn't in the tent when we heard the noises."

"Or when that thing came in and attacked us," Mandy added.

I pulled my notebook out of my shirt pocket and started a new page.

Suspect: Tricia Norton.

Motive: To scare us.

"Why would she do it?" I asked Carol and Mandy.

"You heard her crying to go home," Carol said.

"She never wanted to come in the first place," Mandy added.

"Hmmmmm." That made sense. I added to my notes:

Motive: To go home early.

Clues:

I sighed. I still had no clues.

I looked over to where Tricia was sitting by herself, making faces at her plateful of beans and franks. "Tricia looks lonely," I said. "I think we should go over and talk to her."

"Please," Mandy said. "I'm trying to enjoy my lunch."

Carol agreed. "No wonder she's lonely," she said. "All she does is complain and — "

I waved my notebook at them. "It won't look so suspicious if we *all* go over and talk to her," I said.

I sat down next to Tricia. Mandy sat next to me. Carol sat next to Mandy, as far from Tricia as she could get. We all smiled, big forced smiles. "Hi!" we said at the same time.

Tricia eyed us suspiciously. "What do *you* want?"

Mandy licked her lips. "Great lunch, huh?"

Tricia scowled at her plate. "Do you *know* what they put in hot dogs?" she said. "Snouts and tails and — "

I set my plate on the ground. "Uh — some excitement we had last night, huh, Tricia?"

"I didn't get a wink of sleep," she said.

I ignored the complaint. "You were lucky. Not to be there, in the tent. When that creature came in, you know."

Tricia gave me a know-it-all sort of look. "I *told* you not to eat food in the tent. I *told* you —"

The urge to bop suspects was getting to be a habit. I said a quick prayer for patience. "Yeah," I said. "I know." I forced another smile. "Where *were* you, anyway? We were . . . worried about you."

Carol almost choked on her beans and franks.

"I *told* you hot dogs aren't good for you," Tricia told her. "Do you know what — "

I didn't want to hear it again. "Where were you, Tricia?" I repeated.

She gave me the same sort of look she'd given her beans and franks. "Why?"

Mandy had had enough. "Because we think — "

"Because," I interrupted, "we thought maybe you saw something. Something that might help me figure out who was responsible."

Tricia thought that over, then shook her head. "I didn't see *anything*," she said. "I was asleep. In the bus." She started listing her latest complaints. "It was too cold in the tent. And the ground was too rocky. And Carol snores. And — "

"I do *not* snore!" Carol said. She stood up, her half-finished plate of beans and franks in her hand.

I thought this was a good time to end the conversation. I picked up my plate in one hand and took Carol's arm with the other. "I have to go find Nick," I said. "We have to plan our message for tonight."

40

As soon as we were out of Tricia's line of sight, I took out my notebook and wrote:

Alibi: In bus, asleep.

"Well," Mandy asked me. "Did she do it? What do you think?"

I didn't know what to think. "Hmmmm," I said.

CHAPTER 6

Nick and I agreed on the Scripture reading.

We agreed on the message and who was going to say what.

And we agreed not to speak to one another, ever again, when it was over.

That night, my mother decided to let Tricia Norton sleep in *her* tent, with her and Mrs. Henderson.

I slipped out of our tent after dark to say good night to Max, who was still doing guard duty in the middle of the camp. "Keep a good eye out, Max," I told him. I fished a peanut-butter cookie out of my pocket.

"Woof! Woof!" Max wagged his tail. Good old Max, always eager to help with a big case.

I gave him the cookie and went back to the tent. Carol and Mandy had promised to stay awake with me, but they were both sound asleep when I got back. They'd left their sleeping bags unzipped. Their flashlights were shining brightly on the tent floor beside them.

I crawled into my own sleeping bag, held tight to my flashlight, and tried to stay awake. But we'd had a long, busy day — hiking, biking, rock and leaf collecting, playing games, doing camp chores. I found myself nodding off, struggling to keep my eyes open.

Oooooooohhhh! Oooooooohhhh! Screeeeeeeechhh!

I sat up, wide awake. Mandy and Carol sat up beside me.

Screeeechh! Oooooohhhh! Snorrrrtt!

Something tugged at the left side of the tent. Something big and strong. Something else, just as big and strong, pulled toward the right. The tent rocked from side to side.

"Auuugggh!" Mandy, Carol, and I scrambled for the door.

"Open it, Mandy!" Carol begged. "Quick!"

"I can't!" Mandy wailed. "The zipper's stuck!"

Oooooooowwwwwllll! The tent pitched to the right.

Screeeeechh! It was pulled back, jerkily, to the left.

"Auugghh!" Mandy screamed in my left ear.

"Auugghh!" Carol echoed in my right.

I pushed Mandy out of the way. "Let me try it!" I yelled. I tugged and pulled at the zipper until I got it loose. I scrambled out of the tent, with Mandy and Carol clawing their way out right behind me.

44

Dad, Mom, the Hendersons, and the other kids were coming from all directions.

"What happened?" Dad asked. "Are you all right?"

I nodded. "I think so. But something — *something* was shaking our tent."

"Something *big*!" Mandy added.

"It was making weird noises," Carol said.

"Weird *scary* noises!" Mandy whimpered.

I was mad. This joke had gone on long enough. I stomped over to Nick and Greg, who were standing together, grinning at us. "Where were you two when all of this was going on?" I demanded.

Nick smiled, smugly. "I was with your father," he said.

He was *where*? I looked at my dad. Dad nodded. "Nick scratched his hand on some bramble bushes. He and Greg came over for some antiseptic."

46

"I think we should go *home,* Mr. Doyle." whined a voice nearby. "I think we should go home right *now.*"

I turned to my only remaining suspect. "And I suppose *you* were with my mother," I said.

Tricia seemed surprised by my question. "Yes. Yes I was."

Mom nodded.

Some detective work I was doing. My only suspects had my own parents for alibis!

"I wonder why Max didn't bark or anything this time," I muttered, too loudly.

Everybody went with me to check it out. Our fierce and fearless watchdog looked up at us and wagged his tail. Then he went back to gnawing the steak bones somebody had given him.

Everybody laughed. Everybody but me. I smiled. Good old Max. He was always ready to tear into a good clue when he found one.

CHAPTER 7

It was Mr. Henderson's idea to have rowboat races across the lake. Dad was surprised when I asked if Mandy and I could go in the same boat as Greg and Nick — pleasantly surprised. "I'm glad to see you're listening to your own message," he smiled.

That made me feel a little guilty. I didn't tell him I was really listening to a daring detective hunch instead.

Nick and Greg took one set of oars. Mandy and I took the other set. We sat there glaring at each other, waiting for one of the adults to come along and give us last-minute instructions.

"Are you ready, kids? Now remember, you'll have to pull together," Mrs. Henderson told us. "And you'll need to choose someone to give directions." She inspected our lifejackets to make sure they were fastened correctly. "We'll have lunch on the other side of the lake. The first team to get there wins. Good luck — and be careful!"

"*I'll* give directions," Nick and I said at exactly the same time. Then we glared at each other.

I decided not to argue with him. "Fine," I said. "*You* do it." While he was giving directions, I could be working on my case.

Nick seemed disappointed that I'd given in without a fight. "I've seen them do this in the movies," he said. "I'll say 'pull' and then we'll all pull together."

"Fine," I said. I got a grip on the oar handles and waited for Mr. Henderson to give the signal to start.

"Ready! Set! *GO!*"

"Pull!" Nick shouted. "Pull!"

We pulled with all our might. Mandy and I pulled one way. Nick and Greg pulled the other. All the other boats started across the lake. Our boat just went around in circles.

"We have to pull in the same direction!" I shouted.

"I *know!*" Nick snarled. He made a face at me while we all got our oars in position. "Pull!" he yelled.

The boat shot forward in the right direction.

Nick grinned. "Pull!" he said. "Pull!"

We pulled together, working in time to Nick's orders. The boat picked up speed. We began to catch up to the others.

"Nice sweatshirt," I said to Nick between pulls. I smiled. The shirt was way too big for him, like it belonged to somebody else.

It caught him off guard, just like I'd planned. "Uh, yeah," he said. "Uh, pull!"

The boat stalled, then shot forward again. "Pull! Pull!"

"I thought you forgot your sweatshirt," I said.

Greg gave Nick a nervous glance. Nick stopped shouting orders. The boat slowed down again.

"I, uh — borrowed one," Nick said. "From one of the guys." He scowled at me. "Forget the shirt!" he said angrily. "We're going to come in last! Pull! Pull!"

We got back in rhythm. We even passed the boat with Mom, Mrs. Henderson, Carol, and Tricia. It wasn't much of a victory. Mom and

Mrs. Henderson were rowing by themselves. Tricia and Carol were too busy arguing.

"Pull! Pull!" We passed the boat with Janet, Dwayne, Ron, and Shandra. "Pull! Pull!"

"Funny," I said. "That looks just like the sweatshirt your brother was wearing when he dropped you off the other day."

Nick ignored me. "Pull! Pull!"

"You know," I said to Mandy, "Dad said he's going to have Park Security looking around tonight."

Nick lost his rhythm. "Uh, pull! Pull!"

"Dad thinks it's somebody from another campsite," I told her. "He says whoever it is will be in big trouble. He says they could be *arrested*!"

Greg and Nick stopped pulling and looked at each other. Dwayne, Janet, Ron, and Shandra stuck out their tongues as they rowed by. Mom and Mrs. Henderson smiled, too busy rowing to wave. Carol and Tricia were still arguing.

"We're going to be last, Nick," I reminded him.

"Huh?"

I pointed to the boats ahead of us. Some of them had already reached the other shore. "Mandy and I can't do it by ourselves. We really should pull together," I said.

CHAPTER 8

Those who didn't have kitchen duty had a little free time before dinner. I wasn't surprised when Nick and Greg decided to "take a little walk down the trail."

I told Mom and Dad that Mandy and I were going for a walk too. We got the same instructions Nick and Greg had gotten: "Stick to the trail. Stay together. Dinner's in an hour. Be careful."

"And take Max with you," Dad added.

My faithful bloodhound was a great assistant. But he wasn't very good at sneaking up on suspects. While Mandy and I slipped quietly from bush to bush, trying to keep out of sight and keep an eye on Nick and Greg at the same time, Max trotted through the woods, sniffing logs and digging at tree stumps, making enough noise to be heard back home in Bayside.

A squirrel raced up a tree trunk and Max started barking. Mandy and I ducked down, quick, and pulled Max down beside us.

Nick and Greg turned around and stared in our direction. I held Max's muzzle and prayed he wouldn't bark again. "He's just anxious to catch up to the culprits," I whispered to Mandy.

"Yeah, right," she grumbled.

Greg shrugged at Nick. Nick shrugged at Greg. They started down the trail again. When they were nearly out of sight, we followed after them.

They came to a signpost and turned off into the woods. When we got there, I read the sign.

Baker Street Campsite. I smiled. "You know," I said. "Like in Sherlock Holmes?"

Mandy wasn't much of a mystery reader. "If you say so," she said.

As we crept closer to the campsite, we could hear loud music and smell cooking meat. Max forgot all about logs and tree stumps and squirrels. He began tugging at his leash, hurrying me down the trail.

"Good old Max," I whispered. "Always anxious to wrap up another big case."

Mandy took a big whiff of the steak-scented air and smiled. "Yeah, right," she said.

We tiptoed up to the bushes at the edge of the campsite. Nick's brother Barry didn't seem all that surprised to see him. "What'd you forget now, Squirt?" he asked Nick.

Nick made a face at the name. "Nothing. We came to warn you. Darcy's dad is going to call Park Security. I *told* you that you guys were going too far. You should have stopped after the first night."

I had planned to make a big entrance — to spring out of the bushes and yell "Aha!" I'd even practiced it earlier in my tent, using my best daring detective voice. But good old Max couldn't wait. He saw the culprit standing there, with a plate full of steak in his hand. Max charged out of the thicket, dragging me behind him.

"*Maaaax!*" I yelled as we flew past Nick and Greg. Max leaped, full force, on Barry.

Barry's friend, Joel, took off running. Thanks to good old Max, Barry never had a chance to escape. Max and the steak plate went one way. Barry and I went another. Max ended up on the plate. The steak ended up in Max's mouth. Barry landed on his rear. And I landed on my hands and knees in front of him.

I peeped out at him through my tousled hair. "Ha ah!" I said.

"What?" Barry said.

"*AHA!*" I corrected myself. "Caught you red-handed."

He glanced at his palms. "Huh?"

I got up and dusted myself off. "Don't try to act innocent, Barry Rinaldi. You're the one who was making those noises outside our tent. And you're the one who let that — that wild *creature* attack us."

Barry laughed. "Wild creature? That was just Poe. He wouldn't attack a flea." He pointed at the kitten, sound asleep on one of the bedrolls a few yards away.

I could just hear the rest of the kids when they found out our big, furry creature of the night was a scrawny black kitten. "Yeah, well, you're in a lot of trouble when my dad finds out, anyway," I told Barry.

"How's he going to find out?" Barry asked me. "Where's your proof?"

Since he was still sitting on the ground, I could look him in the eye. "You're going to tell him," I said.

Barry snorted and opened his mouth to say something. But Nick spoke first. And to my surprise, he agreed with me. "Maybe you better, Barry," he told his brother. "Mr. Doyle's not so bad. He'll probably believe the girls anyway. And we might not be in so much trouble if we tell him the whole thing."

On the way back to Sleepy Hollow Campsite, I was smiling. "What's so funny?" Mandy asked.

"I was just thinking about all the stuff Barry's going to 'volunteer' to do once Dad gets done with him. Dad — "

I didn't get to finish. Max stopped so suddenly, *right* in front of me, that I bumped into him. His ears went up. He sniffed the air a couple of times. Then he took off after something small, black, and furry, pulling the leash out of my hand.

At first, I thought it was Poe he was chasing. Then I saw the white stripe. *"Maaaax!"* I yelled.

Bright and early the next morning, Greg, Nick, and Barry cooked breakfast for the whole youth group. They even volunteered to wash the pots and dishes, clean up the campsite, and take down all the tents while the rest of us went down to one of the park fields for a game of softball.

On the way home, we rode with all the bus windows open. Not even Tricia Norton complained about the chill. Mom and Dad, Mr. and Mrs. Henderson, and all us kids crowded into the first few rows of seats. Barry, whose friend Joel had left him stranded, rode up front with us. Max had the whole back of the bus to himself.

When we got back to the church, Nick Rinaldi came over and apologized. "It was a dumb thing to do," he said, holding out his hand to shake.

I could have said, "Yeah, it was," but I didn't. I shook his hand instead. "Maybe next time we can win that boat race," I said.

Nick smiled. "Sure we can," he said. "If I'm ungrounded by then. And if we pull together."

It took four days and five baths before Max could sleep in the house again. As soon as he was allowed back in my bedroom, I gave him his share of the fee Mom had paid me — a box of animal crackers. Then I showed him my copy of the camp picture Mrs. Henderson had taken — taped into my scrapbook of important cases solved by Darcy J. Doyle, Daring Detective.

Catch Up on All of Darcy's Cases!

The Case of the Mixed-Up Monsters
Book 1 $2.99 0-310-57921-X

Somebody has been making a mess in the neighborhood, and everybody thinks it's Darcy's pesky little brother. Join Darcy as she gets to the truth.

The Case of the Choosey Cheater
Book 2 $2.99 0-310-57901-5

The big game is coming, and somebody is stealing homework. Darcy thinks the two are linked, but she doesn't have much time to solve the mystery.

The Case of the Giggling Ghost
Book 3 $2.99 0-310-57911-2

Is Mrs. Pendleton's house really haunted? What about all those noises? It's up to Darcy to solve the mystery.

The Case of the Pampered Poodle
Book 4 $2.99 0-310-57891-4

Fifi, the prize-winning poodle, has disappeared—right before the pet show. It takes faithful Max and a special kind of courage for Darcy to solve this case.

The Case of the Creepy Campout
Book 5 $2.99 0-310-43271-5

When things keep going wrong on the youth group campout, everybody thinks Tricia is causing the problems. It's Darcy's job to find out the truth.

The Case of the Bashful Bully
Book 6 $2.99 0-310-43281-2

Nobody can figure out the new boy. Nice one minute, fighting the next. What's going on? It's a race between Darcy and the snoopy school reporter to find out.

The Case of the Angry Actress
Book 7 $2.99 0-310-43301-0

Somebody's rude "practical jokes" could stop the school play. Who is the culprit? It's up to Darcy to find an answer before the play is canceled.

The Case of the Missing Max
Book 8 $2.99 0-310-43311-8

Vacation with Grandma and Grandpa was supposed to be fun, but instead Darcy is frantic. Her faithful dog, Max, has disappeared!